SUPPANDI & FRIENDS

Tinkle mash-up stories have always been at the top of the most-requested list from readers. There's something about seeing Suppandi, Kalia the Crow, Tantri the Mantri, Shikari Shambu and other *Tinkle* Toons in the same story. For the first time ever, we present to you a collection filled with only *Tinkle* mash-up stories!

These include special stories from *Tinkle*'s classic 100th and 200th issues. There's also a special story from Billy Drain the fangless vampire of the comic horror series Dental Diaries, teaming up with Aisha from SuperWeirdos— and so much more!

Plus! Suppandi laugh-out-loud adventures pepper the pages!

The combination of so many *Tinkle* Toons really made this issue bloom. I love seeing my favourite characters together.
Srilekha M., Rajahmundry, *Andhra Pradesh*

It's a good idea to bring our favourite Toons together. That way we get double the entertainment in a single story!
Shivansh A.S.

I love *Tinkle* mash-up stories. I eagerly await more such mash-ups.
Tapasya Marathe, *Mumbai*

MARCH OF THE TINKLE BRIGADE

Script: *Dev Nadkarni* and *Iyer Prasad B.*

Illustrations: *V.B. Halbe*

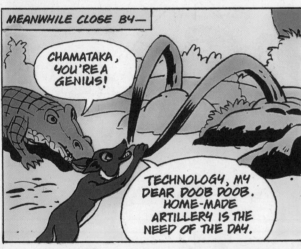

... AND THEN I'LL BE THE KING INSTEAD OF THE KING...

FIRE!

ZING!

BUMP!

LET'S GO AND SEE IF WE HIT ANYTHING.

HULLO! WHAT HAVE WE HERE?

GROAN!

A MAN.

DOOB DOOB, SEE IF YOU CAN BRING HIM ROUND.

I'LL TICKLE HIM WITH MY TAIL.

...AA...

TICHOO!

WHAT HIT ME?

HEH HEH! I DON'T KNOW. YOU WERE OUT COLD AND WE HELPED YOU COME TO. HEH HEH!

I SAY, YOU LOOK FAMILIAR. HAVEN'T WE MET BEFORE?

AH, YES....

WE'VE MET IN **TINKLE.**

YOU'RE CHAMATAKA AND HE'S DOOB DOOB.

...AND YOU'RE TANTRI!

5

THANKS FOR THE GOOD TURN YOU DID ME. NOW WHAT CAN I DO FOR YOU?

OURS IS A TALE OF WOE...

...AND ALL BECAUSE OF ONE FEATHERED FOE.

WHO'S THAT?

KALIA THE CROW.

CAN YOU HELP US GET RID OF HIM?

AND A SINISTER PLOT IS HATCHED—

REST ASSURED. I'LL FINISH HIM OFF FOR YOU.

EXCELLENT!

HEY, THERE'S KALIA HAVING A DRINK...WRING HIS NECK, FRIEND.

THAT SHOULDN'T TAKE LONG.

JUST THEN—

?

SWISH SWISH

6

7

* Now Mumbai

MEANWHILE BACK IN THE FOREST—

9

...AND SOMEWHERE IN THE PROCESSION—

KEECHU I'M HUNGRY.

DON'T FRET. THERE'S SOME DELICIOUS GRASS UNDER THOSE COCONUT TREES.

HEH HEH. THOSE FOOLISH RABBITS.

I DON'T LIKE THE WAY CHAMATAKA'S EYEING US.

HEH HEH, I RECKON I'LL GET THOSE RABBITS NOW.

COME HERE, LITTLE RABBITS.

GO AWAY. GO AWAY.

MEANWHILE—

AH! THE GREAT SHIKARI SHAMBU. I'VE HEARD A GREAT DEAL ABOUT YOUR EXPLOITS. I'VE ALSO HEARD THAT YOU'RE A CRACK SHOT.

HEH HEH, SO I AM.

...BUT I DON'T BELIEVE IT.

WHAT?

10

SEE THAT CHAP ON THAT COCONUT TREE? WATCH ME GIVE HIM A SCARE.

BUT—

EEE...

ROAR!

BANG

OH NO, I'M FALLING! SOME IDIOT HAS CUT THE ROPE!

I'LL GET YOU NOW.

SOB SOB

HEY, BOY. WHAT'S THE MATTER? COME, TELL ME ALL ABOUT IT AND I'LL HELP YOU.

SUPPANDI TELLS ALL—

WHY, THE ANSWER'S SIMPLE.

JUST CHANGE HANDS. TRANSFER THE GROUNDNUTS FROM YOUR LEFT HAND TO THE RIGHT...

...AND THE DAL FROM THE RIGHT HAND TO YOUR LEFT AND THERE YOU ARE.

CLAP! CLAP!

BRAVO, HODJA. JUST WHAT WE EXPECTED OF YOU.

AND NOW WE MOVE ON.

14

AND AFTER MANY HOURS OF TREKKING...

...AND FLYING...

...THEY ARRIVE IN BOMBAY.

WHEN —

WHERE'S MY GUN? MY GUN... IT'S GONE!

HOW CAN I FACE THE WORLD WITHOUT MY GUN?

I DON'T HAVE IT.

WHERE COULD IT HAVE GONE?

IT'S NOT WITH ME.

NOR ME.

NOR ME.

IT WAS ON YOUR SHOULDER.

WHERE COULD IT GO?

HEY, SUPPANDI, WHAT ARE YOU DOING?

IT'S NOT HERE.

WHAT'S NOT HERE?

16

*The Tinkle office in the year 1986

SUPPANDI
X-Ray

Story & Script:
Dolly Pahlajani

Pencils & Inks:
Archana Amberkar

Colours:
Umesh Sarode

Letters:
Pranay Bendre

SUPPANDI! THE NEW X-RAY MACHINE I HAD ORDERED HAS JUST ARRIVED. I WANT TO TEST IT... COME ALONG!

OKAY, SIR.

IN THE X-RAY ROOM—

PRETEND YOU'RE THE PATIENT. LIE DOWN HERE.

I'VE PLACED THE PLATE UNDER YOUR LEG. LIE STILL NOW...

HEY! WHERE ARE YOU GOING, DOC?

BEHIND THAT DOOR, I'LL TAKE THE X-RAY FROM THERE SO THAT THE RADIATION DOESN'T GET TO ME. EXPOSURE TO X-RAYS IS HARMFUL, YOU KNOW...

19

Put on Your Party Hat!

Story & Script
Dolly Pahlajani

Art
Abhijeet Kini

Letters
Prasad Sawant

Dear Star of Tinkle,
Your presence is requested on November 14 at the Casa Evala for an evening gala. Please enter before 8 p.m. so that you don't miss the main event that will change your life forever.
Yours in anticipation,
Your Host

ULP!

BANG!

NOW IS THAT TIME WHEN YOUR LIFE CHANGES...

...MY DEARIES!

(PHEW!) RELAX, GUYS. IT'S JUST A SWEET OLD LADY WITH WINGS.

ThumP

EHEHE... SORRY, SUPPANDI.

NO PROBLEM. BUT COULD YOU MOVE YOUR HANDS PLEASE? I TOOK LOTS OF PAINS WITH MY HAIRDO TODAY.

HMMMM... WE SHALL HAVE TO DO SOMETHING ABOUT THOSE THREE STRANDS YOU CALL A HAIRDO. BUT FIRST...

...LET ME INTRODUCE MYSELF. I'M MADAM LORTAI AND I'M YOUR FASHION FAIRY GODMOTHER. I'M ALSO A HUGE *TINKLE* FAN AND SO, I DECIDED THAT I WOULD MAKE *TINKLE'S* STARS BEAUTIFUL AND FASHIONABLE.

OH, I THINK WE'RE FASHIONABLE ENOUGH.

SO AM I!

BAH! HUMANS KNOW NOTHING ABOUT FASHION! VAMPIRE COUTURE IS AGELESS.

REALLY? YOUR CLOTHES NEVER GROW OLD? WHAT DETERGENT DO YOU USE?

NO, DEARIE... I THINK HE MEANS THAT VAMPIRES DON'T BOTHER CHANGING THEIR CLOTHES NO MATTER HOW OLD THEY GET.

I KNEW SOMETHING SMELLED ROTTEN IN HERE.

UH, SORRY. THAT WOULD BE ME. I HAVE COME IN STRAIGHT FROM THE FIELD...

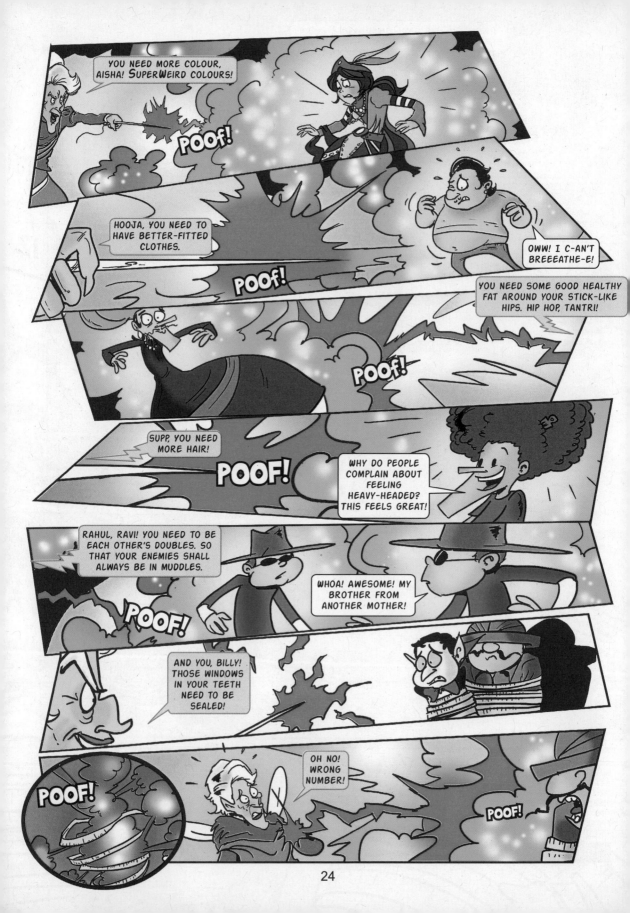

24

25

OOMPH!

THIS IS MY PARTY! AND NO ONE IS GOING TO SPOIL MY MAKEOVER PLANS.

NOW, FOR YOU, I WANT A DASHING, MODERN COSTUME.

POOF!

WHAT'S THIS?! I DIDN'T ASK FOR A HAT FOR YOU! LOSE THE HAT!

POOF!

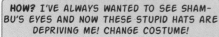

HOW? I'VE ALWAYS WANTED TO SEE SHAMBU'S EYES AND NOW THESE STUPID HATS ARE DEPRIVING ME! CHANGE COSTUME!

POOF!

POOF!

NO! MY MAGIC IS FAILING ME! WHY?!

LOSS OF FAITH IN OWN MAGIC. YOU ARE GETTING A TICKET FOR THAT. COURTESY THE SOUL-SEARCHER'S MAGIC FAITH REVIVAL COMMITTEE.

FINE

NO-NO! I DON'T NEED REVIVAL OF MY FAITH IN MY OWN MAGIC! I AM LORTAI, THE MOST FASHIONABLE FAIRY IN THE WORLD! YOU CAN'T—

SUPPANDI
Doctor, Doctor, Go Away!

Story
T.S. Karthik

Script
Shruti Dave

Pencils & Inks
Archana Amberkar

Colourist
Umesh Sarode

Letters
Prasad Sawant

UFF! WHO IS RINGING THE DOORBELL SO HARD?

TING TONG TING TONG TING TONG

SUPPANDI! WHAT'S WRONG? WHY ARE YOU OUT OF BREATH AND KILLING MY DOORBELL?

(HUFF-PUFF) MAD— MADDY! QUICK, TELL ME...

WHAT? WHAT IS IT, SUPPANDI?

IS IT TRUE THAT AN APPLE KEEPS A DOCTOR AWAY?

WHAT?! UH... YEAH, IT IS. WHY?

THEN, QUICK! GET ME AN APPLE RIGHT NOW!

BUT WHY?!

YOU SEE, I WAS PLAYING CRICKET AND I HIT A SIXER...

...THE BALL BROKE OUR NEIGHBOUR, DR. DIXIT'S WINDOW, AND NOW THE ANGRY DOCTOR'S AFTER ME!

THAP

SHIKARI SHAMBU FT. MOPES & PURR
FIGHT CLUB

Story & Script
Shruti Dave

Pencils & Inks
Savio Mascarenhas

Colours
Snehangshu Mazumder

Letters
Pranay Bendre

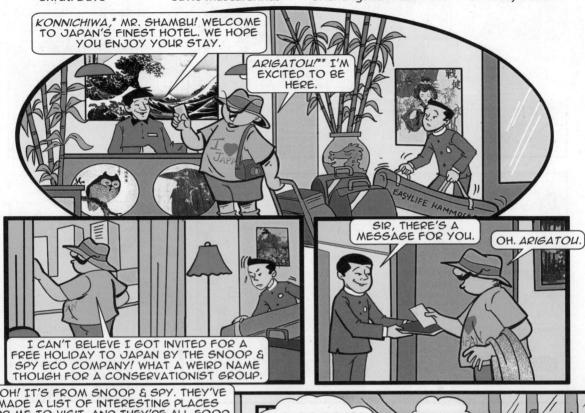

*Hello in Japanese **Thanks in Japanese
#Hello!

GREAT! WE'LL MEET YOU THERE. WE'LL CATCH THESE FOLKS RED-HANDED AND RESCUE THE INSECTS.

ER...

CLICK

THERE REALLY IS NO SUCH THING AS A FREE HOLIDAY.

AHA! SHAMBU DOESN'T KNOW THAT THE SNOOP & SPY ARE MOPES AND PURR UNDERCOVER!

THE PLAN WORKED! WE HAVE THE TIME AND PLACE, SAKI.

LET'S RESCUE MY COUSIN, HAMATO, FROM THE FIGHT THEN, PURR.

DON'T WORRY, WE WILL. THERE'S NO LANGUAGE BARRIER WITH SHAMBU IN OUR TEAM. NOTHING CAN STOP US NOW!

EVENING—

WHERE ARE ALL THOSE SNOOP & SPY PEOPLE? THEIR PHONE LINE IS ALSO DEAD!

湖畔

Miyazaki

(GULP) HERE I AM. I HOPE I GET OUT OF THIS IN ONE PIECE.

31

FIGHT!

FIGHT!

FIGHT!

FIGHT!

THERE MUST BE A WAY OUT! IF SNOOP & SPY DON'T SHOW UP, I'LL BE FIGHTING FOR MY LIFE!

MEANWHILE, OUTSIDE THE CABIN...

THERE'S NO WAY WE CAN ENTER FROM THE FRONT. EVEN IF I BEAT UP THIS GUY, THE GUARD OUTSIDE THE CABIN WILL SEE US.

FROM BEHIND THE CABIN THEN. COME ON!

AND SO—

WELL–WELL–WELL. LOOK WHO'S CRASHING OUR PARTY.

UH-OH. WE HAVE TROUBLE FOR COMPANY.

WHY THAT LITTLE...

HERE WE GO.

WE'RE NOT HERE TO CAUSE TROUBLE. WE'RE JUST HERE TO RESCUE THE INSECTS.

THOSE INSECTS... ARE OUR MEAL. THE LOSERS AT LEAST. HE-HE. SO TURN AROUND AND LEAVE.

MEANWHILE, ON THE OTHER SIDE OF THE WALL—

NUMBER 301 VERSUS NUMBER 420!

NUMBER 420? OH NO! THAT'S MY PET! I'D BETTER SNEAK OUT BEFORE THEY FIND OUT WHAT I BROUGHT!

BUT SHAMBU WASN'T THE ONLY ONE WORRIED...

WHERE IS MY COUSIN AND HIS FRIENDS?! THEY WERE SUPPOSED TO RESCUE ME! I CAN'T FIGHT. I **WON'T** FIGHT!

OH NO! OH NO, NO, NO!

PLEASE DON'T BEAT ME! OH, PLEASE, PLEASE, PLEASE!

THIS MANTIS ISN'T REAL! IT'S A TOY! WHO'S NUMBER 420?

HUH? A TOY? PHEW!

THAT GUY! HE'S THE ONE WHO PUT THE TOY IN. CATCH HIM!

OH NO!

34

35

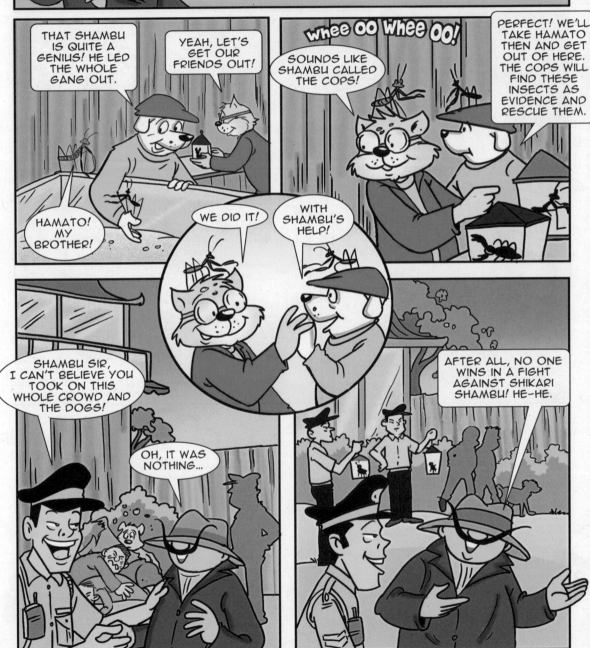

SUPPANDI Plant Protection

Story & Script
Dolly Pahlajani

Pencils & Inks
Archana Amberkar

Colours & Letters
Pranay Bendre

TODAY, JUNE 5, IS WORLD ENVIRONMENT DAY. LET US ALL TAKE A VOW TO PROTECT OUR TREES AND PLANTS. IN RETURN, THEY WILL PROTECT US.

SUPPANDI!

YES, MA'AM.

I'D LIKE YOU TO MEET MR. NARAYAN HERE. HE'S THE MOST FAMOUS SHRUB SHAPER IN TOWN. I WANT HIM TO WORK ON OUR GARDEN. TAKE HIM THERE PLEASE.

RIGHT AWAY, MA'AM.

A HALF HOUR LATER—

HOW'S IT GOING—OH!

SNIP!

YOU SHALL NOT PASS!

STOP! WHAT'S GOING ON HERE?!

YOUR HELPER, HE'S LOCO. HE'S NOT LETTING ME SHAPE YOUR SHRUBS!

BUT, MA'AM, IT'S WORLD ENVIRONMENT DAY.

I HAVE TO PROTECT OUR PLANTS.

WHY, YOU! WASTING MY PRECIOUS TIME! GRRRR! PROTECT YOURSELF NOW!

I DON'T NEED TO! THE PLANTS WILL PROTECT ME!

SWAT!

OW!

SEE! THEY DID! NOW IT'S MY TURN AGAIN!

I'M TOO OLD FOR THIS. ⋝SOB!⋞

SUPPANDI ROAD RULES

Story & Script	Pencils & Inks	Colours	Letters
Shruti Dave	Archana Amberkar	Umesh Sarode	Prasad Sawant

42

Mopes & Purr feat.
Shikari Shambu in TRAINED DOGS

Story & Script	Pencils & Inks	Colours	Letters
Neel Debdutt Paul	Savio Mascarenhas	Akshay Khadilkar	Prasad Sawant

AT THE SEMINAR FOR URBAN ANIMAL STUDIES...

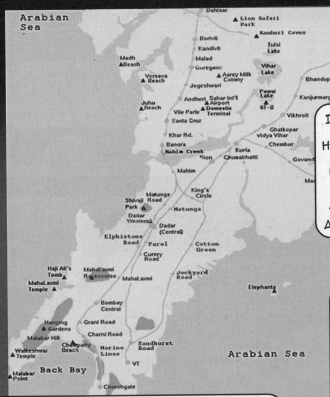

IF IT WEREN'T FOR MY FRIENDS, I WOULD HAVE MISSED IT TOO. I AM VERY GRATEFUL FOR THEM. AND I AM VERY GRATEFUL TO YOU FOR GIVING ME THE OPPURTUNITY TO ADDRESS YOU TODAY.

A FEW MONTHS AGO, I FOUND A WEBSITE WHICH CHRONICLED DOGS ON THE **MOSCOW METRO RAILWAYS.** RESEARCHERS, BLOGGERS AND COMMUTTERS HAD NOTICED A PATTERN AMONGST THEM.

DOGS HAD DISCOVERED THAT FOOD WAS AVAILABLE AT THE CITY CENTRE DURING THE DAY, AND THERE WERE ABUNDANT SUPPLIES IN THE SUBURBS AT NIGHT. THEY HAD MASTERED THE METRO SYSTEM, LEARNED HOW TO FOLLOW TRAFFIC LIGHTS, FIGURED OUT HOW MUCH TIME IT TAKES BETWEEN STATIONS, AND LEARNED TO COUNT BETWEEN THEM. THEY WOULD TRAVEL, JUST LIKE THE MASSES OF THEIR FELLOW HUMAN CITIZENS ACROSS THE CITY, FOR A BETTER MEAL.

AND THEN I DISCOVERED THAT YOU DIDN'T HAVE TO TRAVEL ALL THE WAY TO MOTHER RUSSIA TO OBSERVE THIS.

A FEW MOMENTS LATER...

IT STARTED A FEW MONTHS AGO. IN FACT, IT WAS BATE THAT SHOWED US THE WAY.

BATE?

WE HAD BEEN LIVING IN BANDRA FOR THE LAST 14 YEARS. AND ONE EVENING IT STRUCK ME.

PLEASE USE ME!

THE HUMANS GO TO THE CITY DURING THE DAY, AND COME BACK TO THE SUBURBS AT NIGHT. IF WE FOLLOWED THEM, CAN YOU IMAGINE THE AMOUNT OF FOOD WE WOULD GET?

SOUNDS LIKE A GREAT IDEA.

SO SONALI AND I STARTED FOLLOWING THEM. WE REALIZED THAT'S WHAT THOSE TRAIN THINGYS ARE FOR. THEY GO FROM ONE PLACE TO ANOTHER.

WE STUDIED THE TIMINGS OF THE PEOPLE. WE LEARNT HOW TO STAY AWAY FROM THE BOXES IN WHICH ALL THE GOOD SMELLING PEOPLE WENT. FIRST-CLASS KICKING THEY GAVE US. BUT WE FOUND A DIFFERENT BOX EVERY DAY.

I WANT TO SEE THIS.

SURE. COME WITH US.

47

BACK OFF, HUNTER MAN!

OH CUTE DOGGY DOG DOG!

HEY, THIS GUY IS THE FATSO WHO HELPS ANIMALS, RIGHT? WHAT'S HIS NAME? SHIKARI, SOMETHING. **SHAMBU!** THAT'S RIGHT!

AWWWW. CUTE DOGGIES. WHAT ARE YOU DOING ON THE TRAIN?

MAYBE HE CAN HELP US. WHAT DO YOU SAY?

HERE, LITTLE ONES. COME EAT BISCUITS.

SUDDENLY...

GAH! ITS THOSE DRATTED DOGS AGAIN!

I'D LIKE TO REPORT DOGS ON THE TRAIN AGAIN... WE ARE BETWEEN BANDRA AND KHAR. COME SOON.

HEY! YOU THERE! GREEN MAN. WHY ARE YOU FEEDING THEM? THEY'RE DISGUSTING STREET DOGS. AND CAT.

LET THEM BE.

OH, I'M GOING TO LET THEM BE ALL RIGHT. LET THEM BE IN CAGES FOR THE REST OF THEIR MISERABLE LIVES.

WATCH OUT!

RUN!

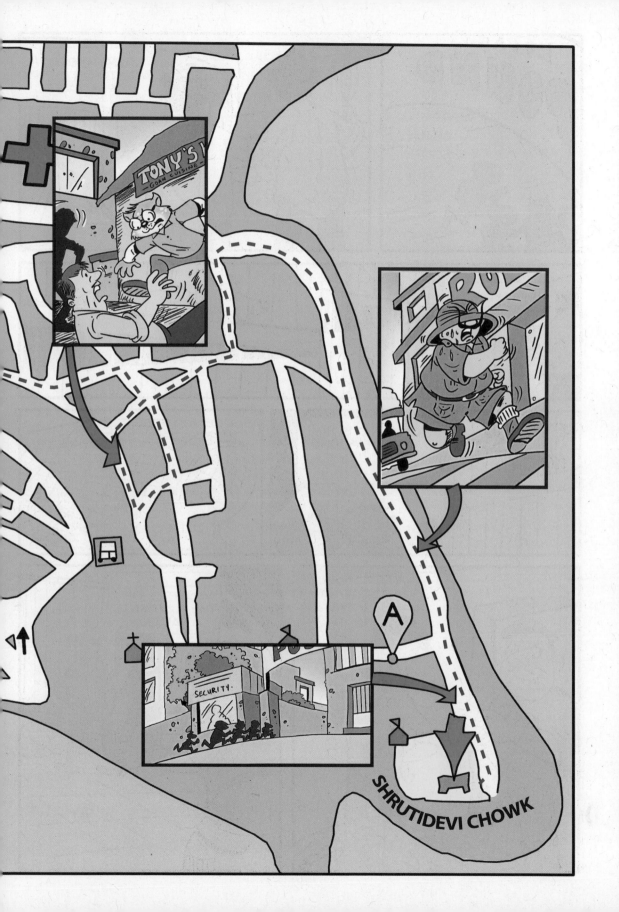

LOCAL POUND

AH HA!

JUST WHERE WE WANT YOU. STUPID CREATURES!

HEY! AKBAR! THERE HE IS!

WOW! THAT'S HIM! WOW! WE **FOUND** HIM! I CAN'T BELIEVE IT!

SUDDENLY!

HEY! OUCH! LET GO OF ME!

GOTCHA!

STUPID MUTTS!

WHAT DO WE DO ABOUT THE CAT, THOUGH?

LET GO... (PANT)... OF THEM... (PANT) (PANT)...

53

STRANGER SIGHTINGS

Story & Script Sean D'mello

Pencils & Inks Vineet Nair

Colours Umesh Sarode

Letters Pranay Bendre

GREAT! WE'RE ALL HERE. WE NEED TO HUNT FOR THIS STRANGE CREATURE THAT HAS AIZWA SPOOKED.

I HAVE A KINGDOM TO CONQUER, PEOPLE! I DON'T HAVE TIME FOR SILLY NONSENSE!

WILL YOU QUIT DOING THAT, TANTRI?!

DUSHTA'S LATEST SMOKE GRENADES MAKING YOU NERVOUS, SHAMBU?

GUYS, QUIT KIDDING AROUND! WINGSTAR'S RIGHT! EVEN I'VE READ THE REPORTS. WONDER IF IT'S SOME SUPERWEIRDO?

I SHOULD HAVE BROUGHT MOMMY ALONG!

FINE! LET'S DO THIS THEN. I NEED TO GET BACK TO MY PLANS IN HUJLI. HERE'S WHAT WE'LL DO... BUZZ... BUZZ...

WHY ARE YOU FALLING BACK, SHAMBU? ARE YOU SCARED TOO?

ME? YOU'RE THE LILY-LIVERED FANGLESS VAMPIRE, BILLY DRAIN! I JUST DON'T FEEL LIKE SHARING MY SNACKS!

=HMPH= YOU—

THUMP

HUH? WHERE DID BILLY GO—

ZOOP

ZOOP

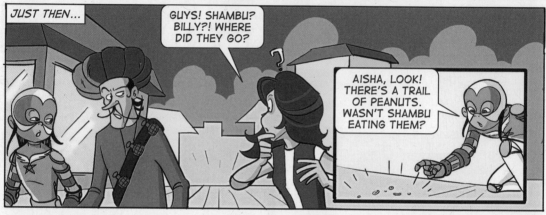

JUST THEN...

GUYS! SHAMBU? BILLY?! WHERE DID THEY GO?

AISHA, LOOK! THERE'S A TRAIL OF PEANUTS. WASN'T SHAMBU EATING THEM?

THE TRAIL LEADS TOWARDS THE RELEK FOREST! LET'S GO.

AMAZING! FIRST, I WASTE TIME ON SUPERSTITIOUS NONSENSE. NOW I GET TO BABYSIT A GROWN MAN AND AN OVERGROWN BABY!

SOMETIME LATER...

THE TRAIL ENDS NEAR THE DOOR OF THAT HOUSE.

PLEASE HELP ME. PLEASE!

HELP ME!

HUH?

MINUTES LATER...

GOTCHA!

THERE!

LET'S GO! WE HAVE NO TIME TO LOSE!

=GASP=

THE POOR BABIES! THEY ARE ALL TIED TOGETHER. WHO WOULD DO THIS?

WHY, THAT WOULD BE ME!

RASHA! BUT... DIDN'T THE PHEICCHAM KIDNAP YOUR FAMILY?

YOU GUYS ALSO LED ME TO THE LAST PHEICCHAM. SOMETHING I WAS HOPING YOUR FRIENDS SHAMBU AND BILLY HERE WOULD DO! THAT'S WHY WE KNOCKED THEM OUT.

HA! AND YOU BOUGHT MY STORY! I NOW HAVE ALL THE PHEICCHAMS AND THE TINKLE TOONS UNDER MY THUMB!

SHAMBU! BILLY!

TIE THEM ALL UP! THE PHEICCHAMS WILL GRANT EVERY LAST ONE OF MY WISHES. FIRST AIZWA, THEN MIZORAM, THEN INDIA, AND THEN THE WORLD. ALL UNDER MY FEET! MUHAHA!

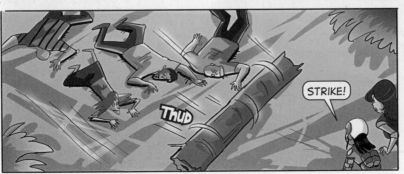

Say 'Cheese'!

Story & Script Sean D'mello

Art Sahil Upalekar

Letters Prasad Sawant

HUH? WHERE AM I? HOW DID I GET HERE?

AAAAH!

SOMEONE HELP MEEE!

AAAAH!

NO WAY! SHIKARI SHAMBU, RIGHT IN FRONT OF MY EYES!

THUD

I NEED TO FOLLOW HIM. WHERE THERE'S SHAMBU, THERE'S ALWAYS ADVENTURE!

PHWEEE

THUMP

MINUTES LATER—

YOU OKAY, KID?

UMM, YEAH, I THINK SO. MY HEAD JUST RINGS A BIT. WHAT HAPPENED?

TANTRI, MY DEAR TANTRI! COME MEET THIS GIRL WHO JUST SAVED MY LIFE.

Rustle Rustle

=HMPH= I SAW, YOUR HIGHNESS. YOU WERE LUCKY SHE WAS AROUND.

IT'S TANTRI THE MANTRI, IN THE FLESH! YOU KNOW, YOU'RE TALLER IN PERSON.

WHAT DO YOU MEAN BY "IN PERSON"? HOW DO YOU KNOW ME?

OH, NEVER MIND. IT'S QUITE A LONG STORY!

WHATEVER THAT *TINKLE* WRITES ABOUT ME IS ALL HOGWASH!

I'M HUNGRY, TANTRI.

YOUR HIGHNESS, I HAVE A BANANA.

=HMPH= YOU'D THINK SHE WOULD HAVE OFFERED ME SOMETHING TO EAT TOO!

THANK YOU, LITTLE GIRL.

SUPPANDI, GIVE ME THE CAP FOR THE CAMERA, PLEASE.

SUPPANDI!

65

66

THE END

SHAMBU DECIDED TO TACKLE THE PROBLEM AT ITS SOURCE—

NOW, COULD YOU ALL EXPLAIN TO ME EXACTLY WHAT'S BEEN GOING ON WITH THE GOATS?

GONE! ALL GONE!

THEY COME AT NIGHT!

WORK OF A SNOW LEOPARD!

NOT A LEOARD, THE YETI!

WITH FANGS LIKE KNIVES!

ALL RIGHT, THANK YOU. BUT YETIS ARE NOT REAL. THE SNOW LEOPARD, HOWEVER, I SHALL SEE TO.

AND I PRAY THAT THE SNOW LEOPARD IS JUST AS IMAGINARY!

AND SO SHAMBU'S GETAWAY TURNED INTO A WORKING VACATION—

(GASP) (HUFF)

WHY DON'T I EVER LEARN MY LESSON AND JUST KEEP MUM?!

HOURS LATER—

UH-OH, IT'S GETTING DARK. MUTTON OR NO MUTTON, THE HOTEL SOUNDS LIKE A GOOD IDEA.

⇒SNIFF SNIFF⇐ I SMELL HUMAN...

GRRR

RAAARRRR

AAAH!

MEANWHILE, MOPES AND PURR WERE CONDUCTING THEIR INVESTIGATION— THESE GUYS WILL TELL YOU WHAT'S BEEN HAPPENING AROUND HERE.

OOH! I CAN'T WATCH!

BUT THEN—

YEOWWW!

THAT'S RIGHT! DON'T YOU EVER COME BACK!

JOB WELL DONE, SHAMBU OLD CHAP! HE-HE-HE!

ANOTHER PROBLEM SOLVED! AND NOW I'M OFF!

LOOKS LIKE WE'VE FOILED YOUR PLANS AGAIN, DABOO.

THIS TIME WITH A LITTLE HELP FROM THE FAMOUS SHIKARI SHAMBU!

PHOOEY! IF THAT LEOPARD HADN'T BEEN SCARED OFF, I WOULD HAVE BEEN FREE!

AND WHAT, OR WHO, EXACTLY SCARED THE SNOW LEOPARD OFF? OUR HEROES WILL NEVER KNOW THE TRUTH...

SSSHHH!

BUT WE WILL!

ATTACK FROM OUTER SPACE

Script : Prasad Iyer

Illustrations : V.B. Halbe

DEEP IN SPACE AN ALIEN CRAFT MAKES ITS WAY TOWARDS OUR PLANET.

PLANET EARTH APPROACHING, YOUR MAJESTY.

GOOD. PREPARE TO HOVER OVER THE SURFACE AND CAPTURE SOME SPECIMENS FOR EXAMINATION.

WE MUST KNOW WHAT SORT OF CREATURES INHABIT THIS WORLD BEFORE WE SET OUT TO CONQUER IT.

IT WILL BE DONE, MIGHTY KING BLINKOR.

WE ARE HOVERING 500 METRES ABOVE THE SURFACE.

GOOD. NOW LOOK FOR CREATURES WE CAN CATCH WITH OUR ENERGY RAY.

MEANWHILE IN TINKLELAND, HOME OF OUR FRIENDS —

HEY, KALIA!

WHY, HELLO, KEECHU.

KEECHU, YOU'VE BECOME VERY PALE. DON'T BE AFRAID. CHAMATAKA ISN'T AROUND...

HELP, KALIA!

HE – HE'S DISAPPEARED! WHAT'S HAPPENING!

SQUAWK! SQUAWK!

A CHICKEN! WHAT'S A CHICKEN DOING HERE?

IT'S NO CHICKEN. IT'S JUST SUPPANDI.

SUPPANDI, YOU IDIOT! WHAT ARE YOU SQUAWKING LIKE A CHICKEN FOR?

I HAVE A PROBLEM, KALIA.

MY BOSS IS ALWAYS TELLING ME TO SAVE MONEY. TODAY HE SENT ME TO BUY A FEW CHICKENS.

GO ON!

BUT I GOT A BRILLIANT IDEA. "SUPPANDI", I SAID TO MYSELF, "WHY DON'T YOU BUY A FEW EGGS AND HATCH THEM YOURSELF? THAT WILL REALLY SAVE MONEY AND PLEASE THE BOSS TOO."

AND THAT'S WHY YOU WERE SQUAWKING LIKE A HEN, BECAUSE THE EGGS WOULDN'T HATCH!

HOW DID YOU GUESS?

NEVER MIND.

HEY, WHERE DID HE GO? HE'S DISAPPEARED LIKE KEECHU.

THAT'S THE SECOND SPECIMEN, WE'VE CAUGHT, YOUR MAJESTY.

HE DOESN'T LOOK VERY BRIGHT, THIS EARTHLING. OUR CONQUEST OF EARTH SHOULD BE A WALK-OVER.

CHECK THEIR BRAIN-POWER ON OUR BRAINOSCOPE.

IT'S INCREDIBLE!

THIS LITTLE RABBIT SHOWS MORE BRAIN-POWER THAN THIS FELLOW.

HMM... SO THE BIGGER THEY ARE THE MORE STUPID THEY BECOME. LOOK FOR MORE SPECIMENS.

WHAT'S YOUR NAME?

SUPPANDI.

PERHAPS THATS WHAT THEY CALL FOOLS ON EARTH!

THERE ARE THREE MORE ON THE GROUND BELOW.

GET THEM.

HEH! HEH! I'LL FINISH OFF HOOJA TODAY!

SHONAR IS A SITTING DUCK.

79

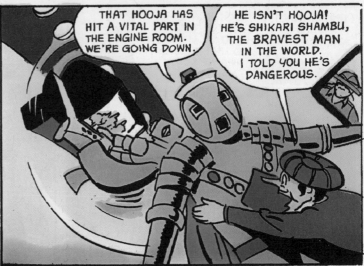

IT'S RANJHA AND HIS MASTER!

RANJHA! TRACK! SCENT!

COME ON, HOOJA! COME ALONG WITH US. WE'VE GOT TO SAVE OUR FRIENDS.

THERE'S THE SPACESHIP! LOOKS LIKE THEY'RE CARRYING OUT REPAIRS.

I'VE BEEN WATCHING THEM FOR SOME TIME NOW. MY DART MUST HAVE HIT SOME VITAL PART AND THAT MIGHT HAVE BROUGHT IT DOWN.

HEY! THERE'S HODJA!

HODJA! THOSE ALIENS HAVE CAPTURED KEECHU AND SUPPANDI.

MAYBE EVEN TANTRI, CHAMATAKA AND DOOB DOOB.

WE MUST SAVE THEM BEFORE THE SPACESHIP LEAVES EARTH.

RELAX! THEY AREN'T GOING ANYWHERE.

WHAT DO YOU MEAN?

I SPOTTED THE VALVE ON THE FUEL TANK AND LET ALL THE FUEL OUT. SO THEY ARE TRAPPED.

BRAVO, HODJA!

MEANWHILE INSIDE THE SPACESHIP—

NOW WHAT?

IT'S MOOSHIK!

AND THE CAT!

I'LL BITE DOOB-DOOB'S HAND. WHEN HE LASHES OUT WITH HIS TAIL HE IS SURE TO GET THE CAT.

I'LL GET YOU, YOU DIRTY RAT! YOU BIT ME!

YOU STUPID CROCODILE!

AS USUAL DOOB DOOB HAD MISSED.

YOU THERE! HEY! DON'T FALL ON THAT SWITCH!

YOU'LL ACTIVATE THE GIANT MAGNETS ON THE WALL.

DANGER

THE SPACE MAN'S WORST FEARS CAME TRUE. BY FALLING ON THE SWITCH, GUPPANDI HAD ACTIVATED THE GIANT MAGNETS. THE IRON ARMOUR OF THE SPACEMEN GOT STUCK TO THE WALLS.

CLANG   CLANG

CLANG CLANG CLANG

WHAT WAS THAT? IT CAME FROM INSIDE THE SPACE-SHIP!

LET'S FIND OUT!

THEY'RE TRAPPED— ALL OF THEM!

'WERE' DO YOU GO?

Story & Script
Dolly Pahlajani

Art
Abhijeet Kini Studios

Letters
Pranay Bendre

NOW COMING TO WHY I NEED YOUR HELP... I DUG UP SOME HISTORY ON KOUTA AND FOUND THAT HE WAS A SUPERWEIRDO BEFORE HE WAS BITTEN BY A WEREWOLF.

HOW DID YOU FIND THAT OUT? SUPERWEIRDOS ARE NOT VERY FORTHCOMING ABOUT THEIR POWERS.

I SPOKE TO THE WEREWOLF THAT TURNED HIM. NOW, AISHA, YOU'RE THE ONLY SUPERWEIRDO TRACKER IN THE WORLD.

UH... WELL... IN THE WORLD?

YES! AND WITH YOUR AMAZING POWER, YOU CAN CERTAINLY JIGGLE THIS GUY OUT OF HIS HIDEOUT BEFORE FULL-MOON NIGHT.

NO ONE HAS EVER CALLED MY POWERS AMAZING.

I CAN SEEK HI—

...WAIT A MINUTE! FULL MOON NIGHT IS TOMORROW!

POOF!

THEN YOU'D BETTER HURRY. I'LL BE BACK TOMORROW, AT TWILIGHT. TOODLES!

THE NEXT EVENING—

POOF!

WELL-WELL, LOOK WHAT THE SMOKE DRAGGED IN.

A PUNCTUAL, FANGLESS VAMPIRE.

WHAT'S THIS LOUDMOUTH DOING HERE?

I'M RIGHT HERE, YOU KNOW.

I NEED HEER WITH ME. YOU DON'T GET A SAY.

FINE. BUT DON'T EXPECT ME TO PROTECT TWO DAMSELS FROM THE WEREWOLF.

OH REALLY? HOW ABOUT...

...PROTECTING YOURSELF FIRST?

SCREEEEECH!

AAAAAARGH!

NEED A HAND THERE, *DAMSEL*?

NO THANKS. HUH.

IF YOU BOTH ARE DONE BICKERING, CAN WE MOVE? IT'S GETTING DARK AND I HAVE HOMEWORK TO DO WHEN I RETURN.

SO, HEER AND I WENT INTO THE WOODS THIS MORNING.

IT TOOK US SOME TIME TO FIND YOUR GUY. BUT FIND HIM WE DID.

A HALF HOUR'S TREK AND—

HAH! NO BIG DEAL FOR MY VAMPIRE VISION.

THERE'S THE TREE ON WHICH HIS HOUSE IS BUILT. IT'S WELL CAMOUFLAGED.

YET IT WAS NOT YOUR VAMPIRE VISION THAT LOCATED KOUTA AND HIS HIDEOUT. IT WAS ALL AISHA'S POWERS.

—VERY GOOD HEARING, YES?

ULP!

AND HEER'S IDEA OF MARKING THE TRAIL LEADING TO HIS HOME.

ALL RIGHT—ALL RIGHT! KEEP IT DOWN, WILL YOU? WEREWOLVES HAVE—

89

HE'S... DOING A SNAKE DANCE!

I FORGOT TO TELL YOU... HIS SUPERWEIRD POWER IS THAT HIS SNAKE-DANCE CAN DO THINGS TO PEOPLE'S—

FAAAAART!

—DIGESTIVE SYSTEMS.

I... UH... DON'T FEEL SO GOOD. I'LL SEE YOU LATER.

HEER! WAIT UP, I'LL COME WITH—

NO-NO! YOU'RE NOT LEAVING ME! LOOK AT THE GUY!

RIP

RIP

THE MOON'S OUT! HE'S CH-CHANGING!

93

SUPPANDI
ELEMENTARY

Story & Script
Sana Khan

Pencils & Inks
Archana Amberkar

Colours
Pragati Agrawal

Letters
Pranay Bendre

SUPPANDI IS WORKING AS AN ASSISTANT TO A DETECTIVE—

AND REMEMBER... YOU'RE WORKING IN A TOP SECRET ORGANIZATION!

OF COURSE, SIR! IN FACT, I'M SO PROUD I GOT THIS JOB...

...THAT I TOLD EVERYONE IN MY BUILDING ABOUT IT!

SHEESH! SUPPANDIIII! WHEN I SAY SOMETHING IS 'TOP SECRET', ABSOLUTELY **NO ONE** MUST KNOW ABOUT IT. IS THAT UNDERSTOOD?

BUT... BUT, SIR...

NO 'BUTS'! NOW OFF TO WORK!

THAT EVENING—

SUPPANDI, TODAY'S OPERATION IS CRUCIAL.

OPERATION? IS HE A DETECTIVE OR A DOCTOR?

WE ARE GOING UNDERCOVER NOW.

BUT, SIR, ISN'T IT TOO EARLY TO GO UNDER COVER?

I GET UNDER COVERS WHEN I GO TO BED AT NIGHT.

SUPPANDI! THIS IS NO TIME TO CRACK JOKES! WE NEED TO CRACK THIS CASE!

BUT... BUT... SIR... IF WE CRACK THIS BRIEFCASE, WHERE WILL YOU PUT YOUR FILES?

AAAARGH! SUPPANDIIIIIIIII! WE NEED TO GET EVIDENCE FROM JAGGU'S COMPUTER. LET'S GO NOW!

AFTER SOME TIME, SUPPANDI AND HIS BOSS RETURN TO THEIR OFFICE...

WE'VE DONE IT! WE'VE GOT ALL THE EVIDENCE WE NEED IN THIS CD. NOW WE CAN NAB THAT CROOK JAGGU!

SUPPANDI, COPY THE CONTENTS OF THIS CD ON THE OFFICE COMPUTER AND LOCK IT WITH A TOP SECRET PASSWORD. DESTROY THE CD LATER. AND REMEMBER, SUPPANDI, NO ONE MUST KNOW THE PASSWORD.

A LITTLE LATER—

SUPPANDI, WHAT'S THE PASSWORD TO THE CD'S CONTENT?

I DON'T KNOW, SIR.

BUT THE INFORMATION IS LOCKED! DIDN'T YOU PUT A PASSWORD?

YES, SIR. BUT I TYPED THE PASSWORD WITHOUT LOOKING.

WHAT?! **WHY** WOULD YOU DO THAT?

I WAS JUST FOLLOWING YOUR INSTRUCTIONS, SIR. I MADE SURE EVEN I DIDN'T KNOW THE PASSWORD. **NO ONE** MUST KNOW, REMEMBER?

AAAAAAAARGH!